-Riepules

HOPPING TO AMERICA

A RABBIT'S TALE OF IMMIGRATION

DIANA PISHNER WALKER
ILLUSTRATED BY ASHLEY TEETS

Headline Kids
an imprint of Headline Books, Inc.
Terra Alta, WV

Hopping To America: A Rabbit's Tale of Immigration

by Diana Pishner Walker

illustrated by Ashley Teets

copyright ©2016 Diana Pishner Walker

To order additional copies of this book or for book publishing information, or to contact the author:

Headline Kids
P. O. Box 52
Terra Alta, WV 26764

Tel: 800-570-5951
Email: mybook@headlinebooks.com
www.headlinebooks.com

Published by Headline Books
Headline Kids is an imprint of Headline Books

ISBN-13: 9781882658596

Library of Congress Control Number: 2016933727

PRINTED IN THE UNITED STATES OF AMERICA

This book is dedicated to my children
Curt, Chris, and Courtney

My mother Anna Allessio Pishner's dream was to write children's books. After she passed, on July 14th 2012, I found a few sentences in a notebook, a beginning of a children's story about a little rabbit named Joby. It was an honor to finish it for her.

Joby and his family were not born in the United States. They were born in the country of Italy. They were an Italian family. Joby and his grandparents, Nonno and Nonna, along with his parents, Mamma Rosa and Papa Luigi, and his two sisters, Annabella and Maria, made the decision to leave Italy and travel on a big ship across the ocean to the United States of America.

They left their home and friends, but could never part with their Italian customs, traditions, and way of life. They were sad and happy at the same time about their new American life.

It took almost a month to get to America. All they could see was water. There was not much food for the bunnies to share and some of the food they had never eaten before— like bananas. The tables were set with a tin cup and a tin plate for each meal.

Many languages were spoken on the ship, not just Italian. All the passengers had to be checked out by the doctors. The doctors mostly looked at their eyes, which Joby thought was just silly because rabbits have great eyesight (thanks to all of those carrots.)

Finally they arrived! All the bunnies moved to the side of the ship to see the beautiful lady in the sky, the Statue of Liberty they called her. Mamma Rosa could not believe her eyes, which were full of tears. The bunnies clapped and cheered. Police bunnies asked all the passengers to get into lines behind the chalk marks. For a little while, Joby's family was separated, but they were lucky enough to find each other again. Some bunnies did not get to stay in the new land and had to travel back to Italy.

The big ship landed on the shores of Ellis Island. They scampered and scurried to grab their suitcases, all the while looking at the tall buildings. The door to America was opened for the Riepule family. It was a strange land. The people spoke English and Papa Luigi did not understand their questions.

There was an American lady at the gate when they arrived who wanted to know how many passengers were in their family. She asked their names and if they needed transportation. She also asked about their passports.

Papa Luigi understood the word passport. He showed the American lady the passports of everyone in the family and they passed through the gate.

Papa Luigi had been writing letters for over a year now to his cousin Dominick who was already living in the United States.

Cousin Dominick lived in a little state called West Virginia. Sometimes he sent pictures to the family back in Italy of his garden and his farm animals, but mostly the pictures were of the beautiful mountainside where he lived and his girlfriend, Sarah, of course.

Cousin Dominick came to meet Joby's family at Ellis Island to take them to their new home in West Virginia. He traveled a very long way to get to Ellis Island in the state of New York.

It was not a very big home for all of Joby's family. The family had to share bedrooms. Mamma Rosa made sure there were enough seats at the table for everyone in the family to sit together at dinner time.

The Riepule family always stopped whatever they were doing to come to the table to share a meal and say a blessing for their food.

The Riepule
family arrived in this
new world in the
heat of the summer.

14

The family worked hard together in their garden. They planted food, especially carrots, to have for the long winter months ahead.

Soon, summer was ending and it was time for Joby and his sisters to go to school.

School? Joby hadn't thought about school and having to make "new" friends in this "new" world.

Mamma Rosa took her children to school on the first day to try to speak to the teachers. She and the teachers mostly just smiled at each other. One teacher pointed to some papers and Mamma Rosa signed our names and hers.

It wasn't long after Joby was settled into his classroom that he made his first friend, Stefano. He soon learned Stefano also came from Italy and had learned to speak English very well. Stefano also loved to play the piano and eat chocolate bars, lots of chocolate bars. Sometimes he wore the chocolate on his school clothes which made Joby laugh.

One day, Stefano asked Joby to come to the park to play baseball.

Joby had no idea what baseball was or how much fun it could be.

After playing baseball, Joby and Stefano taught the other children playing with them how to play Bocce ball.

Joby's sisters were making friends, too. They brought their friends home for Mamma Rosa to teach them how to make *biscotti* and all their friends asked to stay for dinner when they saw that Mamma Rosa was preparing a *tiella* filled with potatoes and zucchini.

Sometimes all of the bunnies in the neighborhood got together for parties, especially for holidays. Everyone brought food. Nonno made his famous juice from the grapes and there was always plenty of carrot cake to go around.

Stefano played the piano and cousin Dominick played the accordion.

Papa Luigi brought out his harmonica.

Annabella danced the *tarantella* and Maria sang. The Riepule family shared stories about life in Italy and their new neighbors and friends talked about life in America.

21

Sometimes, when Mamma Rosa talked about Italy her eyes got teary and Papa Luigi promised her the family would go back someday to visit.

The Riepule family loved springtime the best. All the bunnies stayed very busy during this season. They not only planted seeds in the gardens, they stayed busy coloring eggs, helping Mamma Rosa make Easter bread, and cutting olive branches for Palm Sunday. After all, what bunny doesn't love springtime?

Well, little did Joby and his family know, but Papa Luigi had a surprise planned for them. In a little town called Clarksburg, not far from where the Riepule family lived, there was the *Festival di Pasqua* every year in the spring.

Italian bunnies from everywhere traveled to celebrate *Pasqua* which means Easter. The bunnies danced in the street while music played from the stage. There were many booths that lined the town. There were food booths that served pasta and meatballs, sausage and pepper sandwiches, *giovannis*, pepperoni rolls, *cannoli* and even *gelato*. There was one booth just for *fritti*! The *fritti* were hot fresh fried dough sprinkled with lots of sweet sugar.

Some booths sold shirts and jewelry. Of course there were many game booths for the little bunnies. The older bunnies played bingo.

Papa Luigi announced to his family that he wanted to take them someplace special. They hopped in the car and off they went. As soon as they arrived, Papa explained about the festival and how it was going to be a special place for the family to go every year. Joby tried the food at every booth. He played games with his friends and danced with his sisters, even Nonno and Nonna were dancing and happy.

Mamma Rosa began to cry and when Papa Luigi asked her why the tears in such a happy place she told him she missed Italy even more after she heard the Italian music. Papa Luigi explained this was not all of the surprise.

Joby heard his friend Stefano's voice coming from the loud speaker on the stage. Stefano was asking for Joby's family to come up on the stage for a surprise from Papa Luigi.

Stefano played the piano along with his other friends: Chris, Jule, Darrell, and Mark who played guitars and drums. Sometimes his friend, Denise, sang and Weegie played the tambourine. The name of their band was *Amici* which means friends in Italian. This was so exciting for the Riepule family. They thought the festival was the surprise and now there was more!

When the Riepule family came to the stage they began to see many familiar faces and Mamma Rosa started to cry again. The familiar faces they saw now were their family members who still lived in Italy.

They came to the festival. There were lots of hugs and kisses.

The Riepule family, their family members from Italy and all of their new friends from West Virginia enjoyed the whole day together— eating, singing and dancing. They took lots of pictures.

Papa Luigi told everyone we were all not just *Amici*, now we were all family.

Italian Words To Learn

Pasqua- Easter

Riepule (Ree eh'pooh lay)- a slang term for wild rabbits

Biscotti- cookies

Tiella- a dish

Tarantella- an Italian traditional dance from Southern Italy

Giovanni- a sandwich which includes Italian toasted bread, steak, peppers, cheese, and onions

Cannoli- pastry stuffed shells with a sweet filling

Gelato- ice-cream

Fritti- fried bread dough sprinkled with sugar, or drizzled with honey

Amici- friends